MARGUERITE POLAND

The Wood-ash Stars

ILLUSTRATED BY
SHANNE ALTSHULER

DAVID PHILIP
Cape Town Johannesburg

FOR GALIT AND TALYA
AND FOR MARILYN
WITH LOVE

First published in 1983 by David Philip, Publisher (Pty) Ltd, PO Box 408, Claremont, Cape, South Africa

Published in Afrikaans by Human & Rousseau Publishers (Pty) Ltd under the title *Die Vuurkoolsterre*

© text Marguerite Poland 1983
© illustrations Shanne Altshuler 1983

ISBN 0 908396 98 8

Printed and bound in South Africa by Creda Press (Pty) Ltd, Solan Road, Cape Town

THE WOOD-ASH STARS

Once, long ago, a small band of San (also called Bushman) hunters lived near a water-hole far off in the desert wastes. There, each family built its fire and its low shelter of branches and grass.

Early in the day the men would prepare their delicate small arrows, poisoning the shafts, and go off hunting. While they were gone the women and young girls would take their digging-sticks, tie their karosses around them and walk out together to look for tsama melons, mongongo nuts, tsin beans and all the other roots and fruits they gathered for their food.

When they returned in the afternoon to cook what they had gathered, the children and young girls would play games, using a hard round tsama melon as a ball. Then they would sing and stamp as they threw the melon to each other.

They could sing many different songs as they played: the song of the grey loerie bird that calls 'kuri mama, kuri mama', and the song of the wasp and the slow puffadder. But Xama, who was young and whose hair was decorated with loops of ostrich-eggshell beads, would sing her own lament — that she, of all the young girls, wore an old and ragged kaross. What she wanted most was a kaross that was sleek and new, made of soft gemsbok skin. Her old one had holes in it through which the small, cold fingers of the wind crept. Wearing it, she felt as shaggy as a brown hyena.

As she sang she hoped that Gau was listening. If Gau could kill an eland or a gemsbok or a hartebeest with his small poisoned arrows, and make her a kaross, she would surely be the most contented girl in camp.

Gau heard her songs as she stood in the line with the others, tossing the tsama melon back and forth. And though it was the driest time of the year and the herds of buck were scattered so widely across the plains that they were hard to find, he gathered up his bow and arrows and his hunting-bag and went to his brothers and companions asking if they would go with him to hunt.

But this they refused to do, for the hottest winds of summer were blowing that day. The sky was grey with dust. Where, they asked, would Gau find a gemsbok in all that waste, when only the desert scorpions and lizards would be out? So Gau set off alone.

'Where is Gau?' asked the girls.

'Gau has gone to hunt a gemsbok to make a fine kaross for Xama.'

'Ah, ah, ah, ah, ah!' cried Xama, her hands fluttering to her face. 'At such a time!' She looked at the fierce midday sun, afraid of what she'd sung.

All day Gau hunted, finding nothing. Night came. The moon rose up above the hills. He stared at it, thinking that its face was round and light and shining as the face of Xama. Then he took his firesticks from his bag, made a small fire and lay down to sleep.

The next day he travelled on and, at last, he found the prints of many hooves. A herd of gemsbok had passed that way some time before. He followed, trotting now — trotting as a jackal does, intent upon a trail.

At midday, when the sun is fiercest and highest in the sky, he found some gemsbok resting in the shade of thorn trees. Gau laid down his quiver and his bag, stuck a number of arrows in his belt and crept forward, moving slowly towards the herd.

The buck watched him, stamping their hooves every now and then. Closer and closer crept Gau. Then he drew back his bowstring, tight in the notch of the arrow, and fired. And though he knew his arrow had found its mark somewhere in the herd, the buck all turned and stampeded away through the bush.

Back at the encampment Xama waited.

'Xama, come and play the melon game with us,' cried the others.

She shook her head and sat to one side. A day passed. A night. Another day. Already the crickets were singing loudly in the shadows and still Gau had not returned. Xama wept for having sung the song of the old kaross that had sent Gau out into the desert all alone to hunt.

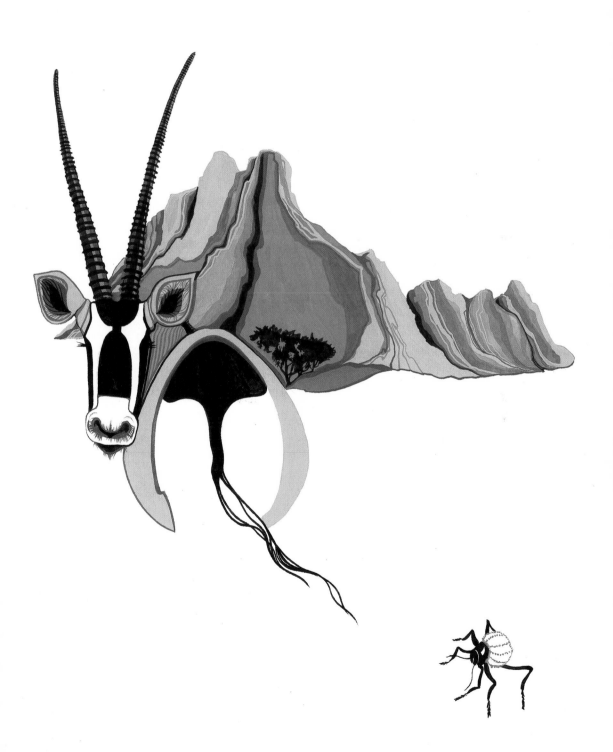

Out on the plains the hunter Gau followed the tracks of the wounded gemsbok for many, many hours. Then he saw — far over the Aha hills — the vultures gathering in the sky. He set out, jogging fast, his arrows rattling in the quiver. When at last he saw the big buck lying dead in the sand, he squatted by it and stroked its smooth skin. He thought of Xama's joy and how she would clap her hands and sing a song of praise. Then he would bray the hide so Xama could fold it softly round her. And she would smile.

Gau could not carry the dead gemsbok away by himself and so he skinned it and cut the meat into strips. These he placed in the skin, which he tied to his carrying-stick. When the sun rose the next morning he set out for home.

But in the time that he'd been gone, the winds had blown up and down the plains smoothing away his tracks in the sand. Gau was young and he could not read the signs of the bush as well as the older hunters. So on he went uncertainly — this way, that way. But no matter which direction he took he saw no sign of his passing — no tree, no stone, no bush that was familiar. The sun came up. The sun went down. It rose again and Gau the hunter, whose thirst was as sharp as the sting of a scorpion in his throat, knew he was lost.

All day he walked. Then towards evening he found a small waterhole. He drank and drank until he could drink no more. But when he picked up his carrying-stick with the gemsbok skin tied to it, and turned away, he knew that not very far behind, something followed silently. Something followed . . . followed on his tracks.

If he walked, so the bush behind him moved a little in his wake. If he stopped to listen, so he knew that something listened too, as if the wind had held its breath. Gau went faster, keeping just ahead of the footfalls in the sand. When night came there was no moon, but from the bush nearby a pair of eyes gleamed in the dark.

Hastily Gau hung his hunting-bag in a thicket, took his firesticks, dragged together twigs and grass and brush and made a flame. Suddenly, into the clearing stepped a huge hyena. It was bigger than any Gau had seen before. It put back its head and howled. Then it stood and watched Gau, whuffling to itself. It shuffled nearer, nose quivering to catch the scent of gemsbok meat. Gau dragged the meat-filled skin closer and stretched out his hand for his bow and quiver. He would drive the hyena away with an arrow.

Then Gau saw, with alarm, that he had left his hunting-bag slung in a bush. He could see it hanging there — out of reach — at the other side of the fire. He shouted at the hyena. But it only stared at him and growled deep in its throat, backing off a little. And as it did, it caught the scent of Gau's hunting-bag. It jumped up on its hindlegs and pulled at the bag with its strong teeth.

It fell with a clatter. The hyena licked at the prints of Gau's meat-smeared fingers on the strap. It scratched at it with a paw and then looked once more towards the gemsbok skin over which Gau sat huddled. It approached, its long shadow creeping towards him in the firelight.

Xama sat outside her mother's shelter and listened to the calls of the night birds. No moon rose. The stars were dim. The wind was fierce and cold. Far off she heard — again and again — the whooping of a lone hyena. Somewhere in the darkness of the plains was Gau the hunter, who had gone to shoot a gemsbok so that he could make a soft, warm, grey kaross for her.

Gau poked the fire and made it blaze. He was afraid. Never had he seen a beast so bold and powerful and unafraid of man. He shifted round the fire, keeping it between the hyena and himself. His arms and legs ached with tiredness but he dared not close his eyes and sleep.

The embers of Xama's cooking-fire glowed softly, for it was late.

'It is the darkness,' she cried. 'There is no light for Gau to guide him home. Oh foolish Gau for going out alone! Oh foolish Xama for wishing for a fine kaross!'

In despair Xama plunged her hands among the coals of the fire. She flung the embers high — as high as she could reach. Again she thrust her fingers in the fire and tossed the fine red ash up into the night.

'Light the way for Gau the hunter!' she cried.

She held her small, burnt hands before her face and wept. The tears stung her eyes and slid painfully between her blistered fingers, cooling them. Then she stared in disbelief as the embers of the cooking-fire she'd thrown in her despair were driven forward by the wind. They glowed in the darkness, stretching out into the desert sky.

11

The hyena crept closer. Gau peered into the dark, looking for a tree into which he might climb with the gemsbok skin. But there was none. The hyena licked its jowls and Gau, not knowing what else to do, threw it a piece of meat — and another, and another, until his store was almost finished. Still the hyena, growing bolder all the time, came nearer.

Desperately Gau threw the last strip of meat. As he did, the sky flared — as embers do when blown suddenly to send sparks scattering. Then, across the sky there blazed a strange soft light. Thousands of little stars burned like wood-ash strewn in the sky. The path of stars arched low — from the far horizon to just above where Gau stood.

The hyena howled and whooped. It cowered low on the sand and stared at the sky, cringing, its lip drawn up above its yellow teeth. Shaking its shaggy head from side to side, it backed away and slunk into the gloom, moaning to itself.

'It is a sign for me!' cried Gau. He leapt up and took his hunter's bag, bow, quiver and carrying-stick and ran, unafraid, following the pathway in the sky.

Xama nursed her burnt and blistered hands. She sang sadly to herself and gazed every now and then at the wood-ash stars she had made. Only in the dawn, when she heard the loud cries of the people, did she leave her brooding and turn and run to where they stood together, pointing excitedly.

There, walking down across the plain, swaggering as if he'd been no further than the waterhole, came Gau. And tied to his carrying-stick hung a gemsbok skin, soft and mauve and grey as a rainy summer sky.

So it was that Gau, the youngest hunter in the band, shot his first big buck and made a warm kaross for Xama, the keeper of his heart.

And so it is — the old ones say — that the thousands of little stars that form the Milky Way are really a handful of wood-ash glowing in the dark. For once a young San girl named Xama threw the embers of her fire into the sky to light the way for Gau the hunter, lost out in the desert wastes in the darkness of the night.

15

THE TALE OF NOMBULELO

Once, on a hillside, high above the river Kei, where the old brown boulders lie scattered and aloes bloom in winter, there lived two children called Mbulelo and Nombulelo.

Their homestead and their father's cattle-kraal lay just below the rim of the hill. In the early morning the red-flanked cattle were driven out into the veld to graze and at dusk the smoke of their mother's cooking fire could be seen drifting up into the evening sky.

Sometimes Mbulelo herded the goats for his father and Nombulelo, his sister, helped their mother in the homestead. She would watch as her mother ground mealies on the old grey grindstone or smeared the floors of the house with a fresh mixture of mud and dung. She would also go down the long path to the river and fetch water, returning with the bucket balanced on her head.

One afternoon the mother of Mbulelo and Nombulelo called them to her and said, 'Go, my children, and collect firewood so that I can cook our mealie-meal and beans. Take the path that leads across the hill and follow it until it forks at a place where an mphanga plant is growing. Listen carefully now,' she said. 'You must take the track to the *right*, for it will lead you to some wattle trees where you will find enough wood to carry home.'

The children nodded and started off.

'Hambani kakuhle — go well, my children,' called their mother.

Mbulelo and Nombulelo hurried past the cattle-kraal. The hoopoe bird watched them from the wall.

'Hoop-hoop, zwiti-zwiti-zwit!

Thez', thez' iinkuni!

Gather, gather sticks!' he cried.

19

They walked along the edge of their mother's mealie-fields where the small grey doves search for fallen grain. Then they ran laughing and chasing each other into the open veld.

On and on they went until they saw the old mphanga plant which stood at the fork in the path. The track to the right looped down to a stand of wattle trees and the one to the left wound up to the crest of the hill where the red-grass bent against the sky.

Nombulelo stopped and looked about. 'Which path is it that we should take?'

'The one to the right,' said Mbulelo.

'No, no!' cried Nombulelo. 'We must take *that* path — the one which climbs towards the sky.'

'Look, there is a sunbird in the mphanga plant,' said Mbulelo. 'See, he wears a bead collar just like mine!' And indeed, the sunbird has a band of bright feathers round his neck as blue as the beads which their mother had bought from the trader's store in the valley.

'Skiz-skiz-skiz!' whistled the sunbird, pointing his beak in the direction of the grove of trees.

'This is the way,' said Mbulelo, 'for the sunbird tells us which must be our path.'

'No,' said Nombulelo. 'We should go to the left.'

'Our mother told us to gather sticks near the wattle trees,' objected Mbulelo.

'*You* may go that way,' said Nombulelo, 'but I shall not!'

And so they parted.

As she climbed the hill, Nombulelo met Ramba, the puffadder who lies in the pathways, coloured like the sand. She stopped, afraid, for Ramba the puffadder strikes as fast as the wind, slow and lazy though he seems. Ramba raised his head and flickered his tongue, waiting for her careless feet to pass.

21

Nombulelo hesitated. 'Perhaps I should turn back,' she said to herself. But oh — how warm the grass was further up the hill, how it bent to the breeze, how the great clouds streamed across the sky. She hurried by, skipping out of Ramba's reach — and he watched her with his narrow yellow eyes.

Up and up she climbed until she reached the crest of the hill. Then down the furthest slope she raced, where the aloes grow red among the rocks.

She found no firewood — for where, on an empty hillside, with only the dry aloe husks tapping together in the wind, will a child find a stick to light its mother's fire? But Nombulelo did not care. She ran and played, exploring the gullies until her shadow was just a little longer than it had been and the wind that had raced with her was colder. She turned back along the path — unsure of her direction.

She clambered up some rocks and stopped, startled, for a crowned hornbill was watching her.

'Kwaa, kwaa!' he croaked.

'Please show me the way home,' cried Nombulelo.

But the hornbill did not answer. He snapped his beak at her and flew away.

Nombulelo scrambled into a dark ravine. She came upon a blue crane with tail-feathers trailing like the plumes of a warrior.

'Show me the way home, Father Crane,' she begged.

'Kraaaark!' he cried and he stalked off, paying no attention to her pleas.

The sun was setting and the rocks hunched dark around her. Nombulelo was afraid. She hurried on, looking for a place where the wind had bent the red-grass against the sky; looking for the path where Ramba the puffadder had lain in the sand; looking for the mphanga plant

22

which would show her the way home. But she could find none of them.

The sun sank lower and the wind blew keen and cold. Nombulelo ran on, crying. The shadows crept in behind her. She heard soft, strange whisperings in the grass. On and on she ran, further and further into the dark ravine. She stumbled and fell.

A small flame flickered in the undergrowth and its smoke was sweet with the smell of roasting mealies. Nombulelo crept towards it. At a three-legged pot, stirring it with a large wooden ladle, sat an old, old woman. She wore a long beaded fringe and the rough fur cap of a diviner and she chanted as she bent to her cooking.

Without looking up the old crone said to Nombulelo, 'Ah, small one, I have heard you coming a long time — for do not lost calves bleat and stumble when they are searching for their kraal?'

'Yes,' agreed Nombulelo fearfully.

'Come,' the diviner beckoned her. 'Taste!'

Nombulelo knelt, eyes cast down and the old one, peering between the beads of her fringe, sat and watched as Nombulelo ate. Then she leaned across and pinched Nombulelo's cheek between two bony fingers. 'Disobedient calves who wander have a wooden prong tied to their necks to keep them in the fields. Children who disobey their mothers are given tasks they must complete before they are rewarded!'

'Yes, Grandmother!' whimpered Nombulelo.

'See,' the old woman thrust a grindstone and a small basket of mealies at her. 'You must grind these very fine. When you have finished, I will show you the way home.'

'Yes Grandmother,' said Nombulelo meekly, eyeing the basket. It was not large. It was not even full. It would take no time at all to grind the mealies fine. Nombulelo took the grindstone, stripped the cobs and set to work.

'Sila, sila, sila! Grind, grind, grind,' she sang. 'Sila, sila, sila! Grind, grind, grind!' she chanted, working slower, for her arms were small and not as strong as she had thought.

'Sila, sila, sila!' she panted, wiping her face, which was damp with her efforts.

The old woman sat by the fire. She smoked her pipe and gazed at Nombulelo through the drifting smoke.

'Sila, sila, sila!' puffed Nombulelo, so intent on her task she did not notice the old woman replacing each mealie she had ground with another, taken from the folds of her cloak.

Nombulelo looked into the basket. The number of cobs remained the same no matter how fast she worked. She began to cry.

'Grind!' The old woman prodded her with her pipe. 'Grind, or I shall not show you the way home!'

And so Nombulelo returned to her task and the old one sat in the firelight.

Not long after he left Nombulelo at the fork in the path where the mphanga plant grew, Mbulelo her brother entered the grove of trees where their mother had told them to gather wood. He collected a bundle, tied it together with a strip of bark and returned homewards. He hesitated when he reached the mphanga plant, wondering if he should climb the hill and search for his sister. But he saw Ramba the puffadder lying in the sand, quiet as dust.

'She must have gone home,' said Mbulelo to himself. 'For who would dare pass Ramba in the path?' But when he arrived at the homestead, it was deserted and only his mother's fowls pecked about the yard and his father's lean brown dog lay in the shade of the wall. He went a little way down the hill and there, below him, at a pool beneath the waterfall where the small waters of the Mvemve stream meet the great waters of the Kei, Mbulelo saw his mother with her bundle of washing.

'Mama, Mama,' he cried. 'Is Nombulelo with you?'

'No, my child,' she said. 'She is not here.'

'She took the path', said Mbulelo, 'that forks to the left of the mphanga plant.

'Hayi-bo!' cried his mother. 'That is disobedience indeed!'

'And see,' said Mbulelo, 'the sun is setting and she will be alone in the dark.'

'Come,' said Mbulelo's mother, placing her washing in a basket and lifting it to her head. 'We must try and find your sister.'

So they set out along the path that leads to the mphanga plant. The dog went ahead, nose to the ground, searching for the footprints of the child.

Down in the ravine the small Nombulelo was still grinding mealies.

'Sila, sila, sila!' chanted the old crone, nudging Nombulelo. 'Grind, grind, grind!'

Slower and slower went Nombulelo, the heels of her hands smarting from the rub of the grindstone. Slower and slower and slower until, unable to continue, she crouched down beside the fire and fell asleep.

The old woman smiled to herself and knocked out the ashes of her pipe against a log — a small sound, like a woodpecker tapping on a tree.

The morning star is the last to leave the sky. It is called the milking star for it stays to light the way for those who milk the cows. It is as bright and warm as the first cooking-fire of the day. But no fire warmed the hearth in Nombulelo's home and no one went to tend the cows waiting in the kraal. For Nombulelo's mother and her brother Mbulelo still searched for her among the hills, calling as they pushed their way through thickets:

'Nombulelo, Nombulelo,
Yiza, yiza mntan'am.'

28

When Nombulelo woke she gazed around her in alarm. Where was the basket of mealies and the grindstone? Where was the old woman who had chanted as she bent to stir the cooking-pot? They had gone, and only a black-eyed lizard watched her from a stone.

Nombulelo scrambled up the hillside and paused, panting, where the first light of morning met the shadows of the valley. There were voices on the wind. Frightened, Nombulelo stopped to listen. From the dark ravine came the sound of faintest laughter. She climbed on hurriedly, glancing back every now and then in fear. Then suddenly, above her, a dark shape appeared on the brow of the hill. Nombulelo crept behind a rock, hid her face in her hands and wept.

As she wept, she heard familiar voices calling, calling:
'Nombulelo, Nombulelo.
Yiza, yiza, mntan'am.'
She peered timidly over the rock. Above her, dark against the morning sky, stood her mother and her brother Mbulelo. Mbulelo bounded
down the slope towards her, while her mother waited for them on the
ridge. Nombulelo ran to her, her arms outstretched as Mbulelo and
the hunting-dog capered round them.

Wearily they turned for home, taking the path that forks beside the
old mphanga plant. Nor did Nombulelo turn to gaze back up the hill
where the wind bends the grass across the sky — for it somehow seemed
to chant, 'Sila, sila, sila, Nombulelo!' And the sound of quiet laughter
was never far behind.

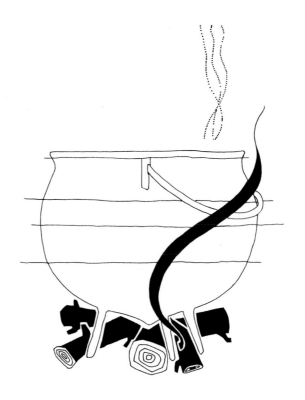

TOBANE AND THE WATERMELON

Tobane, his brother Muzila and their friends drove the goats out into the veld beyond the fields of mealies, pumpkins and beans. When they passed the smaller gardens where the groundnuts and watermelons grew, they stopped and asked old Ma Mawewe, the diviner's wife, if they could have a watermelon to eat.

'Greetings!' said Muzila politely, for he was the eldest.

'Greetings!' echoed the small Tobane.

'Please, Mamana,'* continued Muzila, 'may we who herd the goats have a melon? We get hungry and thirsty out in the bush.'   *Mother

'What?' cried Ma Mawewe sourly. 'Do you think I am working here, breaking my back, for vagabond children to eat my melons?' She shook her hoe at him.

'We will chase the birds from your fields if you will let us have one.'

'You boys are worse than all the birds in the bush! Always begging from hard-working people! Be off!'

The boys turned away disappointed and Ma Mawewe counted her melons as though a troop of monkeys had passed by.

'Mean old woman!' muttered Muzila. 'She guards her melons like a chicken guards its eggs.'

By midday the boys were very hungry and some searched for mice to roast on the small fire they had made. Tobane was left to watch the goats while Muzila and the older boys set bird traps in the grass.

Some months before, the boys had hidden a big, cracked pot in a bush, hoping to attract wild bees. And indeed, within a few days a swarm had nested there. Soon the combs would be rich and thick with honey. The boys were waiting for the time when they could take the first piece from their secret hive.

35

'Muzila,' said Tobane, 'when will the honey be ripe?'

'Soon,' said his brother. 'In a day or two we shall see how much there is.'

'I am hungry,' said Tobane.

'So are we!' agreed the others.

'Well then,' said Muzila. 'Let us steal a watermelon from Ma Mawewe's field.' He stirred the embers of their fire and continued. 'We shall lead it away as one leads a goat!'

'What do you mean?' asked the other boys eagerly.

Muzila laughed. 'Ma Mawewe will not believe her eyes!' he cried. 'Come, let us make a string and I shall show you how to catch a watermelon.'

He stripped some fronds from a nala palm, pulled the fibres from the leaves and rolled them together to make a strong, twisted string.

'We shall send Tobane,' said Muzila.

'But,' protested Tobane, 'Ma Mawewe is working in her garden. She will see me.'

'She will suspect nothing if you tell her that you are looking for a strayed goat.'

'She will beat me with her hoe!' cried Tobane.

'Who cannot run faster than Ma Mawewe?' scoffed Muzila. 'Now, Tobane, take this string and this little knife. Find the ripest melon that you can. Cut the stalk. Tie one end of the string to it and the other to your ankle and then walk slowly away, dragging the melon behind you.'

Tobane shook his head.

'Go, Tobane, or *we* shall beat you,' said Muzila sternly.

One boy stayed to tend the goats while Muzila and the others followed Tobane to the garden where Ma Mawewe was gathering groundnuts.

The boys hid in the grass and watched as Tobane carefully approached the melon patch. Ma Mawewe had her back to him. She was singing as she worked. Some way down the row of plants Tobane spied an enormous watermelon, its leaves fluttering in the warm wind.

He crept towards it. He took out his knife and cut it from its vine. Then he carefully tied one end of the nala string to the stalk and the other to his ankle.

'Hey, mufana*?' cried Ma Mawewe, catching sight of him. 'What are you doing in my garden? Are you after my sweet potatoes?' She waddled towards him, flourishing her hoe.

Tobane was unable to run with the melon tied to his leg. Ma Mawewe would surely catch and beat him. He licked his lips nervously. He could hear the others laughing and wriggling together in the grass. Suddenly he sat down on the melon and peered at his foot, screwing up his face as if he had been hurt.

'I have a thorn in my foot, Ma Mawewe,' he cried. 'It bites deep as the sting of a wasp. I came to look for a strayed goat,' he continued hastily. 'I thought it might have wandered into your garden.'

Ma Mawewe stood over him scowling, her hands on her hips. 'Be quick, mufana, and go!'

But Tobane dared not move. He was afraid she would see the string tied to the stalk of the big green watermelon on which he sat.

'I think,' he said, flustered, 'that the goat may be in those bushes over there.' He pointed down to where the rows of sweet potatoes grew. 'I must chase it out.'

'There is no peace from boys or goats!' complained the old woman, stamping off to peer into the bush. She found nothing so she glared back at Tobane and shouted, 'Hey boy, find your goat and go! I do not want to see you here again or I shall tell your father to beat you.'

Ma Mawewe turned away, her hoe across her shoulder, still mutter-

37

ing with indignation. She returned to her work and Tobane hurried from the garden.

The length of the string unwound as he walked. He reached the grass at the edge of the field and the string pulled taut. He jerked it with his foot. The watermelon was heavy. He pulled a little harder until it bounced from its resting-place. Slowly, so slowly, Tobane dragged the melon behind him.

He ducked down beside the bush where the others hid. Together they drew in the line. 'See, we *can* lead the melon like a goat,' whispered Muzila triumphantly.

Just then, Ma Mawewe looked up from her work. She stared. She clicked her tongue and stared again: a watermelon was moving across her field, all by itself!

Ma Mawewe took a step forward and stopped. The melon rolled across a hummock of earth, slid into the grass and was gone.

'Baloyi*!' shrieked Ma Mawewe. 'Wizards have bewitched my garden!' She ran puffing towards the village, calling wildly for her husband, the diviner.

*sorcerers

'Come and see how watermelons walk away by themselves!' she cried. 'Soon the mealies will get up and march off in the night!'

The young women left their work and came to see why Ma Mawewe was shouting. The little children hid behind their mothers' skirts and stared. The old men sitting in the shade of the village tree stopped their talk and turned to listen.

'I have been sure for many days', lamented Ma Mawewe, 'that the baloyi have bewitched my garden — for are not the shells of my ground-nuts often empty as though they had been dug up, eaten, then buried in the sand? And,' she continued, 'has not the wind been wild at night?' She stared about the anxious faces watching her.

'Yes, Mamana,' said the young women softly, and the children crept

39

closer to their mothers.

'Well now,' said Ma Mawewe triumphantly, 'what else but baloyi . . .' and she lowered her voice to a whisper . . . 'what but baloyi could make a melon — such a big melon too, the finest in the garden — walk away alone?'

'Oh Mamana!' cried the women.

'So!' exclaimed Ma Mawewe. 'I shall speak to my husband, the diviner and ask him why wizards should be troubling me!'

Up on the hillside, sitting in the shade of the big marula tree, Tobane and his friends were cutting up their watermelon. How they laughed as Tobane strutted round the clearing, just like Ma Mawewe, protesting that the melons were bewitched.

When the boys had eaten and only the rinds were left, they played their little nanga flutes, made from goat bone, and listened to the murmur of the bees in the broken pot hidden in the bush.

Down in the village, Ma Mawewe sat before her husband the diviner and asked impatiently why she was being troubled. The melons, after all, were his as well as hers. Surely some powerful sorcerer wished to harm them both?

The old man sighed and scratched his head doubtfully and gazed at his wife. 'I think,' he began. 'Is it not possible', he continued slowly, and he peered up at the smoky rafters of the house, 'that someone has simply stolen a watermelon?'

Ma Mawewe snorted impatiently.

'Boys, for instance,' he continued and he looked at her with a small smile. 'Boys have many ways of getting what they want.'

'Thieves!' cried Ma Mawewe indignantly. 'They will make a fool of me to my own husband! I shall catch that child and beat him with a

stick. And all those other boys — I shall beat them too!'

She took a sala-fruit* shell and a stout stick from the back of the house and said, 'I shall gather sand from the footprints of the thieves. You must look at it and tell me which boys — besides the small one — steal from my garden. Then I shall tell their fathers to punish them.' *monkey orange

So saying, Ma Mawewe defiantly left the village, carrying her little sala shell to gather sand from the footprints of the thieves. The old diviner watched her go and smiled to himself.

Up the hill toiled Ma Mawewe, following the tracks of the goatherds. 'Hah!' she muttered every now and then as she bent to fill the sala shell. She heard the goats bleating further up the slope and she hurried along the path towards them. The boys saw her coming.

'Quick,' cried Tobane, 'let us hide where she cannot reach us! Come, let us climb this big tree. She will never see us in among the leaves.'

The boys jostled with each other to be first into the branches.

'Muzila,' whispered Tobane fearfully to his brother, 'she *will* find us — for see, the melon rinds are scattered everywhere and our fire is still burning!'

'Hah!' said Muzila.' Do you think Ma Mawewe could climb this tree and fetch us down?'

The other boys laughed and scrambled higher.

Ma Mawewe panted into the clearing.

'Aha ha!' she cried, pouncing on a melon rind. 'So it *is* boys who are the thieves!'

The boys in the tree peered down delightedly, trying not to laugh, except Tobane who gazed anxiously at the stick Ma Mawewe carried.

'Bafana*,' cried Ma Mawewe. 'Thieves of an old woman's melons! You will not get away with this! I have a sala shell and I have gathered sand from your footprints. My husband the diviner will be able to look at this sand and tell who you are. You will have to confess and be pun- *boys

43

ished!' She stood waiting but only the grass birds chattered in the thickets and the bees that nested in the old pot droned back and forth in the heat.

'Bafana, come here!' commanded Ma Mawewe again. She clicked her tongue and scowled at the melon rind. Suddenly she stood still, head on one side, and listened. She looked about curiously, and then she started to search the grass and bushes around the clearing. The boys glanced at each other, puzzled.

Ma Mawewe moved faster, poking in the grass with her stick. Then she saw what she was looking for. Eagerly she parted the leaves of a bush and peered inside. Wedged among the branches was the big cracked pot the goatherds had hidden for the bees.

'Honey!' murmured Ma Mawewe with delight. She glanced round furtively — but nothing stirred. She gathered a bunch of long dry grass and lit the end in the goatherds' fire.

She approached the beehive with the grasses in one hand and her stick in the other.

She looked about again to make sure that no one was watching and then she held the smouldering grass near the mouth of the pot. The bees milled around, confused by the smoke. Ma Mawewe reached into the pot and pried out a large piece of honeycomb. She threw the grass into the fire and then she tore some leaves from the bush and wrapped the honeycomb inside them.

As she was about to start off down the hill, Tobane, Muzila and the others, hidden in the big marula tree, blew as hard as they could on their nanga flutes.

Ma Mawewe shrieked with fright. She dropped the honey, the sala shell and the stick and, without a backward glance, stumbled down the hill.

'Baloyi!' she shrieked. 'I am indeed bewitched!'

44

When she had gone, the boys swung from the tree, laughing. Muzila picked up Ma Mawewe's sala shell.

'Here Tobane,' he said, 'take this shell and fill it with soil from Ma Mawewe's footprints. When we get home you must complain as loudly as you can that someone has stolen honey from your hive!' Tobane did as he was told while Muzila wiped the sand from the honeycomb and divided it among the boys.

Ma Mawewe's husband, the diviner, was sitting in the doorway of their house when she returned hot and panting from her climb up the hill.

'Have you caught the thieves?' he asked.

'No!' she snapped. 'They had run away.'

'Ah,' he said, 'but it is work indeed to be a goatherd! One gets hungry on the hills. Who would begrudge a boy a mealie cob, a sweet potato or a handful of groundnuts?'

Ma Mawewe shot a glance at him and sniffed indignantly. But he was staring ahead as though remembering something. 'Perhaps', he said, 'you should take a little of my medicine and scatter it around your garden. That will stop the thieves from taking too much. Rub it on the stalk where the stolen melon grew and the thief will have such a painful little finger he will confess.'

He reached over for his bag of medicines and herbs and brought out a small horn filled with powder.

'Take that to your garden, wife. Scatter it around — but remember, there are more than enough melons for all our needs and for small boys who may be hungry!'

When evening came the boys rounded up the goats and drove them home, playing on their nanga flutes as they went. Behind them all walked Tobane. He carried the sala shell filled with sand from Ma Mawewe's footprints.

The goats jostled and bleated at the village gate. Everywhere the smoke of cooking-fires rose in the evening air. The men sat talking together in the bandla, their meeting-place, and someone, somewhere — way behind the ash-heaps — sang softly to herself.

'Weee! Weee!' wailed Tobane. 'A thief has taken the honey from my hive!' Muzila and the others nudged each other and grinned approvingly.

'I cannot think who the thief might be, but I have taken sand from his footprint and I shall ask the diviner to tell me his name!'

Ma Mawewe heard him as she stirred the porridge on her cooking-fire. Hastily she laid aside her spoon and glanced about to make sure that her husband had indeed gone to the bandla with his friends. Then she called out to Tobane as sweetly as she could:

'Mufana, come here.'

'Yes, Mamana,' he said nervously, clutching the sala fruit filled with sand.

She beckoned to him and he approached her fire slowly.

'You say that someone has taken your honey?' she asked softly.

'Yes, Mamana,' replied Tobane.

'Strange,' said Ma Mawewe. She picked up her wooden spoon and dipped it in the porridge again. 'Today, I was sure that sorcerers had bewitched me — for there, a watermelon was crawling out of my garden, just like a tortoise!'

Tobane stared at his feet and said nothing.

'And now, thieves have raided your beehive?'

Tobane nodded and Ma Mawewe stirred her pot more vigorously.

'Do you think,' she mused, 'that the thief who took your honey is the same one that stole my melon?'

Tobane dared not answer.

'No doubt it is!' said Ma Mawewe firmly. 'But have no fear — there is no need to ask my husband to look at the sand you are carrying in that shell. He has given me some magical herbs to sprinkle in my field to keep away intruders. You may have some to put around your beehive and then — if it is raided — the thief will feel an unbearable pain in his smallest finger and know he has done wrong!' And she thrust her little finger right near Tobane's face to make sure he understood.

She took the sala shell from Tobane and gave him the horn of medicine which her husband had prepared.

'This will keep the thieves away,' she said in a whisper. 'Just as it will keep them from my garden! We who are struggling for food must help each other,' she added solemnly.

Tobane took the little horn and thanked her. 'Do you like honey, Mamana?' he asked innocently.

Ma Mawewe pursed her lips and thought. 'Yes mufana, who does not like honey? But there — I have not seen honey for a long time.'

The next morning Tobane, Muzila and their friends took the medicine to where their hive was hidden and sprinkled it around the pot. Then they put a honeycomb inside a sala shell and took it down to Ma Mawewe in her garden.

Tobane offered it to Ma Mawewe and she in turn cut a watermelon for Tobane.

Just then, Ma Mawewe's husband, the diviner, passed by and saw her give the watermelon to Tobane. And when Tobane had run up the hill with the other goatherds, the old man sat down in the shade and shared the honey from the little sala shell with his wife. They ate in silence, staring out across the garden. Then the wise old man turned to Ma Mawewe and he smiled. And strange to say, Ma Mawewe, who always scowled as though she'd sucked a green marula fruit, licked the honey slowly from her fingers, and smiled back.

CHILD OF THE DOVES

Away in the heart of Zululand, where the old Tugela river slides down green and brown as a crocodile between the hills, there lived a head-man called Dumudumu and his many wives.

Among his wives was one whom Dumudumu held more dear than any other. She was young and sweet-natured and beautiful. But as time went on she became thinner and thinner. The sadness she felt was as heavy as a grindstone in her heart for she could not have children.

The other wives of Dumudumu would jeer at her as she passed alone to her fields and say, 'There goes Fikile — she who bears no children, no, not even a crow!'

And in her sadness, the woman Fikile would talk to the birds that nested in the grass and trees around her mealie field. She would even feed the crows that squabbled in her lands, saying sadly: 'Come, creatures of Fikile, and eat.'

Nor did she chase the birds from her crops as others did, for surely there was enough grain for all when she, Fikile, had no child to feed. Among the birds that came to her fields were two emerald-spotted wood doves that would follow as she hoed the rich red earth between the mealie stalks where the pumpkin vines grew, shaded from the sun.

51

One day, as Fikile sat beneath a thorn tree to drink the sour porridge she had brought with her, the two doves flew down and greeted her.

'Vukuthu!' called one.

'Vukuthuni!' said the other.

The woman gazed at them and then, to her astonishment, the first dove spoke. 'Vukuthu! Why are you crying, wife of Dumudumu?'

'Vukuthuni!' added the other. 'You sit so sadly. Why is it, wife of Dumudumu, that you weep?'

'I weep', replied the woman, 'because I have no children. What is a woman without a son or daughter? I am Fikile, the one who cannot bear even a crow.'

'Vukuthu!' crooned the first dove.

'Vukuthuni!' cried the other. 'Fetch the largest pot from your house, and fetch a knife. We shall help you, for you have fed us when we were hungry and did not chase us from your lands.'

The astonished woman hurried home. She found a pot. She found a knife. She returned — almost running — to the field.

'Vukuthu!' called the first emerald-spotted wood dove.

'Vukuthuni!' cried his companion. 'Take the knife and cut your leg.'

Fikile did as she was told and from her leg drew just a little blood. This she smeared inside the clay pot as the doves said she should.

'Gather some cow-dung and bring it to us here,' said the doves.

The woman searched for cow-dung and returned to the waiting birds.

52

Together they carefully sealed the mouth of the pot, leaving it in the sun to dry.

'Vukuthu!' crooned the first.

'Vukuthuni!' replied the other.

'Take this to your house,' they said. 'Hide it away. Speak to no one of what has happened. Do not open it until we tell you or your wish for a child will not be granted. Go well,' they said. And they flew away with a soft, swift rush of wings.

For many moons the woman Fikile kept the pot in the darkness of her house. From the season that is known by the old ones as Mandulo — the time of the stinging hot sun — until the season of Ncwaba, when the moon is called the new green moon because the trees are budding and the young shoots are flowering out of the dry winter earth, Fikile tended the pot. She often held it in her hands, wondering what lay inside its warm roundness.

And then one day when Fikile was sweeping the yard outside her house, the two emerald-spotted wood doves suddenly appeared.

'Vukuthu!' said one.

'Vukuthuni!' greeted the other.

'I see you!' cried Fikile joyfully.

'The time has come to open the pot,' said the birds.

Fikile glanced round to make sure that they were alone. Then she led the way into her house. She watched, her hands clasped eagerly before her, as the two doves pecked at the hard dung that sealed the mouth of the pot.

'Vukuthu!' crooned one.

'Vukuthuni!' sighed the other, as the pieces fell to the floor.

Fikile closed her eyes, hardly daring to look. The doves, perched on the rim of the pot, leaned into it and murmured to themselves. Fikile crept forward and peered between their outstretched wings.

There in the darkness, curled against the warm curve of the pot, lay a baby girl. Fikile reached in and lifted her joyously into her arms.

'Vukuthu! Vukuthuni!' cried the doves.

Fikile sang a song of praise to the doves — to their green-spotted wings and their voices, soft as the sigh of wind.

'You may tell no one of this child,' said the doves. 'She must be the daughter of the night — one that walks with the moon. No one must know she shares this house with you until the time when she is grown and may wear the beads of a young girl who is old enough to marry.'

Fikile promised to obey the doves and when they were satisfied that all was well with her and the child they left the house and flew away.

When the other wives of Dumudumu the headman saw Fikile pass each day and called, 'There goes Fikile, she who cannot bear even a crow!', she would smile to herself and walk away, no longer bowed as though she carried a grindstone in her heart. Many times her husband, Dumudumu, asked her why it was she sang so joyfully to herself and why it was her step was light. But ask as he might, and dear though he was to her, Fikile would not answer his questions.

56

So the years passed and Nomajuba — child of the doves — grew into a beautiful young girl. Her mother marvelled at her, wishing often to show her to Dumudumu her husband. But she remembered her promise to the emerald-spotted wood doves. Because of this, the girl left the house at night only, when the stars were high and the moon was full.

At night she would take her turn to hoe the fields and the moon would follow where she went, glinting on her hoe-blade. On the way home she would draw water from a pool and return with the pot balanced on her head.

Now it happened that the son of a neighbouring chief, who had been out hunting with his friends, had decided to spend the night on the bank of the river, close to where Nomajuba was working in her mother's fields.

The night was hot and the young chief lay awake and listened to the sounds of the dark. And on the wind he heard singing and the faint splash of water as someone bent to fill a pot. He stood up, spear in hand, and crept down the bank. Not far away he saw Nomajuba washing herself in a pool.

Straight-limbed but timid as an impala doe she stood, and her song was as soft as the call of wood doves. Spellbound he gazed at her, and when she turned to walk away he followed her up through the thorn trees and watched as she entered the homestead of her father, on the hill.

When morning came the young chief sent his friends to ask the head-man Dumudumu if he could marry his daughter who walked with the moon. Dumudumu was puzzled by the request and sent for the young chief. The young man came and drank beer with the headman and told him news of the hunt and the places he had been.

At last the headman said, 'I have many daughters. I shall bring them all before you and you must tell me which you wish to make your wife.'

While the young chief and his companions sat in the shade, the daughters of the headman came before him. Their mothers stood to one side staring at the chief's son just as crows sit huddled, waiting for their prize.

But at last the young man stood up disappointed. 'These girls are beautiful,' he said, 'but none of them is the girl I saw, who walked with the moon.'

Just then Fikile came foward and cried, 'Wait, young chief! I shall show you Nomajuba, child of the doves, she who walks with the moon!'

The headman's wives jeered at her.

'Indeed,' said Dumudumu to the chief, 'do not listen to this wife of mine. She does not know what she is saying.'

'She is Fikile,' cried the wives, 'she who cannot bear even a crow.'

But Fikile walked proudly to her house and summoned her daughter Nomajuba. For the first time the young woman came out into the sunlight and walked between the houses, past the astonished wives of Dumudumu the headman.

'It is she,' said the young chief quietly, and his companions stared with admiration.

At that moment the emerald-spotted wood doves flew down from the sky.

'Vukuthu!' cried one.

'Vukuthuni!' called the other.

'This is your daughter, Dumudumu kaMkhize, child of your wife Fikile, she who they said could not even bear a crow! This is Nomajuba, child of the doves, the one who walks with the moon.'

So it was that Nomajuba married the young chief amidst much rejoicing and lived to bear him many sons and daughters. Her mother Fikile was restored as chief wife in the heart of her husband Dumudumu, and even when she was old and could no longer take the path to the fields with her hoe across her shoulder, she would sit at the door of her house and scatter grain upon the earth. Then in the quiet of the morning two emerald-spotted wood doves would appear, alighting at her feet to eat the food which she had given them.

'Vukuthu! Vukuthuni!' they would coo. And Fikile would tell them with pride of her grandchildren, the sons and daughters of the chief and Nomajuba, child of the doves, the girl who walked with the moon.